For Matthew – Clemmie and Toby's
wonderful Daddy xx

Text and illustrations copyright © 2011 Rebecca Elliott
This edition copyright © 2011 Lion Hudson

The moral rights of the author
have been asserted

A Lion Children's Book
an imprint of
Lion Hudson plc
Wilkinson House, Jordan Hill Road,
Oxford OX2 8DR, England
www.lionhudson.com
Paperback ISBN 978 0 7459 6269 6
US hardback ISBN 978 0 7459 6297 9

First paperback edition 2011
1 3 5 7 9 10 8 6 4 2 0
First US hardback edition 2012
1 3 5 7 9 10 8 6 4 2 0

A catalogue record for this book is available
from the British Library

Typeset in 22/30 Garamond Premier Pro
Printed in China January 2012 (manufacturer LH17)

Distributed by:
UK: Marston Book Services Ltd, PO Box 269, Abingdon, Oxon OX14 4YN
USA: Trafalgar Square Publishing, 814 N Franklin Street, Chicago, IL 60610
USA Christian Market: Kregel Publications, PO Box 2607, Grand Rapids, MI 49501

Sometimes

Rebecca Elliott

LION
CHILDREN'S

Clemmie is the best sister.

She plays **cowboys**.

She has enormous hair.

She makes me laugh and sometimes she stays in hospital.

You are NOT allowed to take **pets** in to hospital.

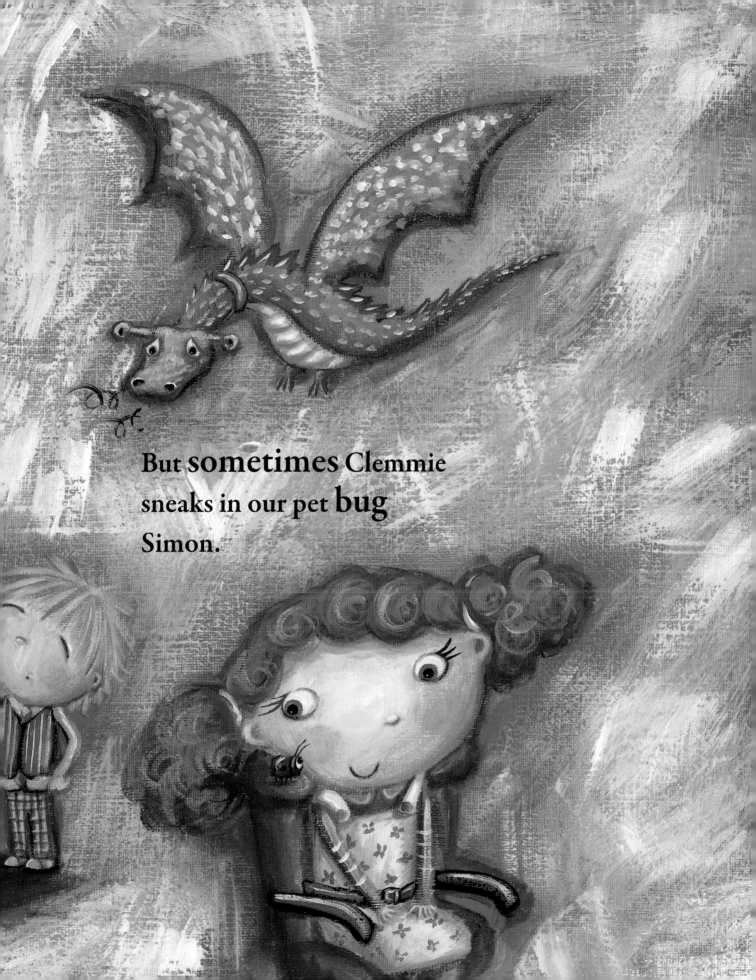

But **sometimes** Clemmie
sneaks in our pet **bug**
Simon.

In hospital Clemmie gets a **bed** that goes

up and **down**

and **side** to **side**,

like a boat.

Sometimes we sail to distant lands on it.

The doctors help Clemmie.

But **sometimes** the doctors need our help.

Clemmie is fed
through a magic
belly tube,
so she doesn't eat
the hospital food.

Sometimes
I eat it for her.

She likes me to eat the

yoghurts,

muffins,

and cheesecakes.

She does not like me to eat the peas.

Sometimes Clemmie has to be **brave.**

And **sometimes** I have to be **brave** too.

Sometimes there's a **playroom** where you can do all the things you like best.

I like to build stuff with blocks,

open and **shut** doors,

and **run** around doing impressions of **elephants**.

Clemmie likes to **stretch,**

watch me,

and look **pretty.**

Sometimes we make lots

and lots

of friends.

And sometimes
we like it to be **just** us.

Sometimes Clemmie gets **very** ill

and I get **very** sad.

But then she holds my
hand **really tightly**

and I know she'll soon
feel better again.

And that makes *me*
feel better again.

When she comes home,
I throw her a **party.**

Clemmie can't **dance** so I do
twice the amount of dancing
to make up for it.

I do NOT
do **tap**
dancing
though.

Well, maybe just
sometimes.

And at sleepytime when I begin to dream of

diggers,

pies,

and slugs,

Clemmie just **cuddles** me really quietly
and waits for me to go to **sleep**.

Clemmie is the best sister and I love her.
And not just **sometimes**.

All times.